SUMMER
Stock

A
NOVELLA

Happy Reading!
Regina

REGINA KYLE

Summer Stock

Regina Kyle

Copyright © 2017 Denise Smoker

ISBN: 978-1546599715
ALL RIGHTS RESERVED
Cover Art: Rebel Book Designs
Formatting: Seaside Publications, ninapierce.com

DEDICATION

For the real Emil Vetrano and for Joan Gustafson, Stephen Ludlow, Joe Treggor, Marty Marchitto, Cindy Simell-Devoe, Cathyann Roding, Toni Cartisano, Mickey Nugent, John Treacy Egan, MaryLee Delaney, Rob and Andrea Kennedy and all the directors who donate their time and passion to introduce young people to the fine art of theater. You're changing lives. Don't ever stop.

One

"What do you mean Emil's not coming?" The heels of Georgi Petersen's character shoes beat a staccato tattoo as she paced the width of the stage, arms flailing. "It's only three weeks until we open. And we haven't even finished blocking the second act."

"I know." Abner Breen, the mayor of Spring Grove and producer for the fourth year in a row of the local theater company's annual musical, nodded his bald head, shiny with summer sweat, in agreement. "But it can't be helped. He collapsed at the Stop 'n' Slurp buying a pack of Slim Jims and a Red Bull. Doc Wolfson says he's suffering from exhaustion. At sixty-five, he's no spring chicken. Doc says if he doesn't slow down – and soon – he's liable to have a heart attack."

"A heart attack?" Georgi stopped her pacing and sank to the stage floor. The smooth, familiar, hardwood was cool under her legs, bare beneath the hem of her khaki shorts. It had always been her safe haven, this stage. The one place where she could become someone else for a few hours at a time and escape the large, loud, dysfunctional mess she called a family.

"I'm sorry, Georgi." Abner's voice floated up to her from the front row, where he sat with his elbows on his knees. "I know how close you two are."

Close didn't even begin to describe their relationship. Emil Vetrano had been her first director, a mentor from the moment she was bitten by the acting bug at age eight, a father figure when her own had died her sophomore year of high school, and a friend when she returned to Spring Grove after college to serve as head of the children's department at the town library.

"I have to go to him." She popped back up to her feet and resumed pacing, the *tap-tapping* of her shoes echoing in the almost empty theater. "Is he at home?"

Abner plucked a handkerchief from the inside pocket of his seersucker jacket and dabbed at his forehead, the pair of ceiling fans whirring overhead not enough to cool even the tiny, 150-seat theater. They'd been trying for years to raise the funds to air condition the building – not to mention complete the long list of repairs needed on the century-old structure – but so far no dice. She didn't want to think about what was going to happen if they didn't meet the town council's deadline.

"They're keeping him overnight for observation," Abner said. "Maybe longer."

"Longer?" Her stomach dropped to her feet.

"Why?"

"You know Emil. Doc's worried if they let him out he'll be back here barking orders at everyone before you could say 'summer stock.'"

True that. Emil didn't much care for being told what to do. Or for sitting still.

Stupid, stubborn man.

"He'll go crazy cooped up without something to keep him occupied besides daytime talk shows and bad reality TV." Georgi headed down the stairs stage left and made a beeline for the seat where she'd left her tote bag. "I'll bring him this week's *Backstage*."

"Georgi."

"And some of those suduku books he likes."

"Georgi."

"Oh, and herbal tea. That's good for calming the nerves, right?" Emil would rebel against giving up his high-test Columbian blend, but she'd force the damn stuff down his throat if she had to.

She swung her bag over her shoulder and started down the aisle.

"Georgi."

The unusually sharp tone in Abner's voice made her stop and turn.

He stood and met her halfway between the stage and the pint-sized box office tucked into a corner at the back of the theater. "There's something I have to tell you before you go."

"Oh, God." She clutched the strap of her bag in a white-knuckle grip. "It's bad, isn't it? Is Emil …?"

"He's going to be fine," Abner insisted. "He's too hard-headed to die."

Her fingers relaxed and the circulation returned to her hand. "Then what?"

"We've found someone to step in as director. He'll be here any minute."

"That's great." She'd all but forgotten the fate of the play in the wake of Abner's revelation. But his latest announcement was a welcome relief, and not just for her and the rest of the cast and crew. No matter how sick he was, Emil would want the show to go on. "Do I know him?"

"You could say that."

"Let me guess." She rested a butt cheek on the arm of one of the seats. "It's Harvey."

Harvey Finn had been Emil's stage manager and right hand man since the dawn of time. He'd never directed before, but he'd be better than no one. Hopefully he'd absorbed some of Emil's brilliance through the years.

"Nope. Not Harvey."

"Please tell me it's not Sebastian." Her co-star had always had aspirations of being the next Orson Welles. And the ego to match. Bad enough she had to pretend to fall in love with him on stage. If she had to listen to him in the wings …

She squeezed her eyes shut and shuddered.

"Not Sebastian either. Although you might wish it was."

"I can't think of anyone in this town I'd rather work with less than him."

"He's not a local." Abner tugged at his shirt collar with one hand, continuing to dab at the ever-increasing pool of sweat on his brow with the handkerchief in the other. "Any more."

A feeling of dread crept like frigid fingers down her spine. "You didn't."

"No." Abner averted his eyes, staring at his shiny cordovan loafers. "Emil did. Called him from the damn ICU."

In a heartbeat, Georgi went from worrying about Emil's recovery to wanting to strangle him herself. Of all people, he should know Jax Donovan was the last person on earth she'd want to spend five seconds with, never mind three plus weeks under his thumb during the run of the show. After all, Emil had been the one to hold her hand and dry her tears when Jax had left her in the dust, throwing aside their plans to attend the state university together for the bright lights of the big city.

"How could he?" She let her bag fall to the floor and kicked at the seat in front of her.

"He didn't have much choice," Abner pleaded. "No one here's qualified to get us up and running in such a short time. And Jax's new show just closed, so …"

"So Spring Grove's golden boy had nothing better to do?" She rolled her eyes. "He couldn't wait to get out of here as a teenager. I can't see what appeal it holds for him now."

"Really?" a low voice drawled from behind her, rolling over her like thunder in advance of an impending summer storm. "I think that would be obvious."

Like a scene in a campy rom com, she turned in slow motion to see Jax lounging against the box office window. The photos in the gossip rags didn't do him justice. Not that she read those things. But it was hard to avoid his too-handsome face, with that sculpted jaw and piercing, gunmetal-blue eyes behind the dark-rimmed glasses he'd worn even before Harry Potter made them trendy, leering at her from the rack beside the checkout counter at Caron's Corner.

He should have been on stage, not behind the scenes, with his movie-star good looks. That's how it had been in high school, when they'd been a couple on the boards and off. Until Jax had split for greener pastures in the form of a spot off the waitlist and a juicy scholarship at NYU Tisch.

And he hadn't looked back since. So why now?

"Doesn't a big Broadway director like you have more important places to be and people to see?"

Abner stuffed his handkerchief back in his pocket. "Jax is here to help his former teacher. Give back to the town that gave him his start. Isn't that right, Jax?"

"You could say that." The man in question crossed his corded arms over a broad chest that strained against the fabric of his Ralph Lauren polo and flashed Georgi a perfectly straight, white-toothed grin. A lock of wavy, chestnut hair fell across his forehead. "Or you could say I came back to get my girl."

Jax shouldn't have been surprised at the stricken look on Georgi's face. But hope sprang eternal, and that's what he'd been consumed with since Emil's call less than twenty-four hours ago had given him the excuse he'd needed to return to Spring Grove.

He stared at her, taking in her sleek, wheat-blond hair, cut shorter than he remembered, her gray-green eyes, bright with annoyance, her full, firm lips, shiny with some sort of gloss, the only sign of makeup he could detect. Not that she needed any, then or now. How was it possible that she'd grown even more beautiful in the eleven years, six months and fifteen days since he'd seen her last?

She ignored him and turned to Abner, hands balled into fists on her trim hips. "See what I mean? I can't work with him."

She jerked her head at Jax.

"Now, Georgi." Abner put a hand on her shoulder, but Georgi shook it off with a glare that could have frozen Dante's Inferno. "Be reasonable. Who else could play your part?"

"What about Martha Ross?" Georgi suggested.

Jax took a few steps down the aisle, stopping just outside of what he estimated to be the range of her throwing arm. Who know what potential weapons she might have tucked away in that monstrosity of a bag at her feet? "If I remember her correctly, she must be about eighty years old by now. A little long in the tooth for an ingénue."

Georgi spun around and focused her icy glare on him. "For your information, she's a very young seventy-five. And I'm surprised you remember anything about this town. You left so fast the proverbial door didn't hit your ass on the way out."

"I didn't have a choice."

She arched a brow at him. "Didn't you?"

Abner backed slowly down the aisle toward the stage. "I'll just leave you kids alone to work this out."

"Stop," Jax and Georgi ordered in unison.

"Imagine that." Jax barely suppressed a smirk. "We agree on something."

"So?"

"So maybe it's a sign."

"Of what?" She crossed her arms in front of her chest, drawing his attention to the sweet, soft curve of her breasts. "That we both want Abner to stay and run interference?"

He made a conscious effort to divert his eyes upward to her face. "That we can find a way to work together."

"Look." Abner cleared his throat. "The rest of the cast should start arriving in a few minutes. Why don't you two take this discussion to the green room? I'll break the news about Emil."

"Fine by me." Jax nodded.

Georgi shook her head so hard he wouldn't have been surprised if it had flown off her neck and into the orchestra pit. "Over my dead body."

"At least listen to him," Abner begged, his voice rising steadily as he went on. "Think about Emil. About the show. About what's going to happen to the theater if we don't …"

"Fine." She cut him off with a wave of her hand. "I'll listen. But that doesn't mean I'll agree."

Georgi spun on her heel, pushed past Abner and made her way back up onto the stage and off into the wings.

"Good luck," Abner muttered, giving Jax a sympathetic look.

Jax shrugged as if to say, "No worries, man, I got this," and followed after Georgi, his feet tracing the familiar path to the green room backstage right. He pushed open the door and found Georgi stalking from one side of the room to the other like a caged tiger.

"Out with it," she snapped the second the door swung shut behind him. "What's the real reason you're here? And don't give me any garbage about wanting to win back 'your girl.' I haven't been your girl since you walked out on me and all our plans and hopes and dreams with barely a so-long-nice-to-know-you."

"Would you believe me if I said I made a mistake?"

She stopped stalking to face him, hands back in fists on her hips. "Damn right you did."

Okay, so she wasn't ready for his grand apology. Not that he blamed her. He'd been a dumb kid, a self-centered asshole who figured she'd be happy to wait for him. And if not, there would be plenty of woman ready and willing to take her place.

He was wrong about the first and right about the second. She hadn't waited, and there had been a whole host of woman standing in line behind her.

But none of them had been Georgi.

Jax crossed the room and sank onto the same battered sofa that had inhabited the space when he was a teenager. He wasn't going anywhere, and he'd learned a hell of a lot of patience in the intervening years. He had three weeks of rehearsal, and one more during the run of the show, to win her over. And he was fully prepared to use every second of it.

Starting tomorrow. Right now, he needed a different approach.

"Emil told me about the town council's ultimatum."

"Thirty days to raise a hundred thousand dollars." She sighed and slumped into the equally ancient armchair opposite him. "They might as well nail the condemnation order to the door now."

"Not if I have anything to do about it."

"So you're going to swoop in and save the day?" She lifted her chin, her smoky eyes narrowing at him. "How big of you."

"I have some investor friends who might be willing to help," he said, choosing to ignore the dig. "If we can convince them the theater's worth saving."

"And how exactly do you propose we do that?"

"Bring them up here. Let them see the place. Learn its history. Watch you all perform." He leaned forward, resting his forearms on his knees. "But we can't do any of that without a show. And we can't do the show without you."

She flinched. "That's hitting below the belt."

He sat back and shrugged. "Just telling it like it is."

"I guess there's a first time for everything."

"Now who's hitting below the belt?" Jax took a deep breath and started again. He couldn't afford to lose his temper. Not with so much at stake. And as important as it was, he wasn't talking about preserving the historic building where he'd spent the greater part of his youth. "Can't we declare a truce for the next four weeks? For the sake of the theater?"

For what seemed like hours but was probably less than a minute, the only sound in the room was the ticking of the old analog clock over the minifridge. When Georgi finally spoke, her voice was quiet but determined.

"On one condition."

"Anything."

"This …" She waved a hand between them. "Is strictly business. Actor/director. Nothing more."

For now. "Naturally."

"I'm not your girl."

Yet. "So you've said."

"And I never will be."

We'll see. "If that's how you want it."

"It is."

She stood and crossed to him, her hand extended. He rose and took it, his calloused fingers engulfing her smaller, softer ones. A zing of electricity shot up his arm and straight to his groin.

"Then we have a deal?" he asked, his voice sounding strangely husky even to his ears.

"We have a deal." She blushed and quickly released his hand.

He smiled at the evidence she was as affected by their brief contact as he was. "Then let's get busy. With the show, of course."

"Of course."

With a curt nod, she turned and left the room. Only when the door had closed behind her did he uncross the fingers he'd been hiding behind his back.

Two

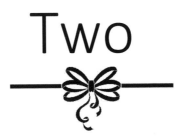

"All right, everyone. Take a break." Jax closed his script and ran a hand through his hair. "Have some water. Grab a bite to eat. But be back here in thirty."

The cast dispersed, their excited chatter bouncing off the walls of the little theater. Georgi stowed her script in her oversized bag, hitched it over her shoulder and followed the crowd toward the exit at the front of the house, anxious to join them for a sip and a snack.

"Except Georgi and Sebastian." Jax's voice froze her mid-step. "You two stay here. I want to work on the kiss scene."

"But I'm starving," Sebastian wined.

"Harvey," Jax called.

The stage manager poked his head out from the wings stage left. "Yea, boss?"

"Can you get Sebastian something from the Kettle?" The Country Kettle, or the Kettle as the locals called it, was just down the street and a favorite with the cast and crew.

"Chicken Caesar salad, dressing on the side." Sebastian barked his order like a drill sergeant. "I'm watching my figure. Nothing worse than an overweight leading man."

He eyed Georgi up and down, his gaze lingering on her full breasts, wide hips and what her mother not-so-lovingly referred to as thunder thighs. His unspoken message was clear.

Except maybe an overweight leading lady.

"Chicken Caesar. Got it." Harvey took a pen from behind his ear and scrawled something – presumably Sebastian's order – on his palm. Ignoring the actor's obvious jab at Georgi, he shifted his attention to Jax. "You want anything?"

"I'm good. Thanks, Harvey." He turned to Georgi. "How about you? Hungry?"

"I brought my own lunch." She pulled an insulated bag out of her tote.

"Still vegan?"

"Not vegan," she huffed, stuffing the insulated bag back into her tote. "Vegetarian. There's a difference."

"I'm sure."

Was she imaging it, or did he just smirk at her?

"Back in a flash, boss. Just text if you need anything else." Harvey disappeared backstage.

Jesus, Mary and Joseph on a *bicycle.* It was bad enough Jax had the entire cast and crew – with the exception of her and Sebastian – eating of the palm of his hand. Even the normally taciturn Harvey was bowing and scraping at his feet.

Barf.

"Now that that's settled, shall we get to work?" Jax leapt up from his chair and vaulted onto the stage, bypassing the stairs. "This scene's not jelling, and we need to figure out why."

"I can tell you why." Sebastian joined Jax on stage, taking the more civilized – but way less manly – staircase. "It's her."

He jerked his head in Georgi's direction. "She hates me."

"I do not hate you." She saved that word for things like Hitler and terrorism and lima beans. Strongly dislike, maybe. "And even if I did, I'm an actress. I can pretend to like you just fine."

"Then why do you stiffen up every time I touch you?" Sebastian asked, pouting like a toddler who didn't want to eat his vegetables.

"I think I see the problem." Jax motioned to her. "Georgie, come on up here."

She dropped her bag and proceeded up the steps

stage left. "Now what?"

"Sebastian, put your arms around her."

Georgi flinched instinctively at the contact. "Is this really necessary?"

"See what I mean?" Sebastian protested. "It's the same thing every damn time. She's like a corpse."

"Insults won't get us anywhere." Jax walked around them, scowling. "But he has a point. Relax, Georgi. Put your hands on his shoulders."

Damn. Sebastian did have a point. She was acting like a spoiled child instead of a seasoned actress. Okay, so unlike Jax she hadn't been brave enough to go for the big time. But she'd performed in more amateur productions than she could count and had acted opposite plenty of prima donnas, a couple of them even worse than Sebastian. She ought to know better. She did know better.

"Sorry." She willed her muscles to slacken and reached up to loop her arms around Sebastian's neck.

"Better." Jax nodded approvingly as he continued to study them with the intensity of Michelangelo surveying the Sistine Chapel. "But still not good enough.

"What's wrong now?" Georgi asked.

"You look like polite strangers," Jax explained. "Which is a step above mortal enemies. But not quite star-crossed lovers."

"How's this?" Sebastian swayed back and forth, pulling Georgi with him.

She tipped her head up to look him in the eye and frowned. "What are you doing?"

"Dancing."

"You call this dancing?"

"It would be better with music."

"You don't need music," Jax interrupted. "What you need is chemistry."

Sebastian stopped swaying, jerking them to a halt. "We're doomed. We've got as much chemistry as a dead battery and a day-old fish. Emil must have been smoking something funny when he cast us together."

Finally. Something Georgi could agree with him on.

"You know what they say." Jax shrugged and smiled. "Fake it until you make it."

"How do you propose we do that?" Sebastian asked.

"It's easier to show you than tell you."

Jax waved Sebastian aside and took his place. Before Georgi knew what was happening, she found herself with his strong arms wrapped around her waist, his chest pressed against her softer one, his scent – a heady mix of soap and sandalwood and sweat – invading her nostrils.

"Wh … what are you doing?" Her voice was husky, her breathing ragged.

"Showing Sebastian here how to create chemistry. First, take her head in your hands, like this."

He put a warm palm on each cheek, cupping her chin. His touch was gentle but firm, like an erotic massage.

"Then look deep into her eyes, like this."

His steely eyes shone with something that looked suspiciously like desire through the lenses of his glasses and his mouth inched closer to hers. Was he really going to … ?

"And last but certainly not least, kiss her, like this."

He'd been building up to it, but that didn't mean Georgi was anywhere near prepared for the inferno that raged through her body when his lips met hers. No sweet, soft kiss, this. Jax had gone straight past smoldering to volcanic, tilting her head and taking her mouth hostage with his lips, teeth and tongue.

Oh, his tongue.

She closed her eyes against his sensual assault and let herself drown in the feel of him, his five-o-clock shadow scraping against her cheek, his broad chest hot and hard under her palms. Holy hell, he was built. The promise she'd seen in the lean, lanky boy had come to fruition in the strong, solid, sexy man.

Everything else disappeared. No stage. No Sebastian. No show.

Just him. Just her. Just them.

Just like high school, when her whole world, her entire existence, had been wrapped up in Jax

Donovan. Until he chose the limelight over love.

If it had ever been love.

No, no, no, no, no. This was not happening. Again.

She pushed against his hard, hot chest.

"Uh, boss?" Harvey cleared his throat. "Food's here."

Jax lifted his head as calmly as if they'd been discussing the weather and not making out like sex-starved nymphomaniacs. "Voila. Chemistry."

You could say that again. Dammit.

Jax stepped back, leaving Georgi suddenly bereft. When he spoke, he addressed all three of them, but his eyes never left hers. "Go. Eat. We'll pick up where we left off after lunch."

"I highly doubt that,"Georgi muttered, tromping down the stairs to retrieve her tote bag as Harvey and Sebastian wandered off in the direction of the green room.

"I'm not going to apologize for kissing you," Jax said, following her.

"Of course you're not," she snapped back. "Just

like you never apologized for leaving."

"You're right. Leaving was a mistake, and I'm here to fix that. But kissing you wasn't."

"What happened to strictly business?"

"That was business." Jax stood in the middle of the aisle with his feet apart, arms crossed over his chest like some sort of superhero.

She faced off with him, hands on her hips. Two could play the superhero game. "So you kiss all your leading ladies?"

"No." He gave her a look that could have melted the iceberg that sank the Titanic. "Only the ones who really need kissing. And sweetheart, you need it bad."

"I … I'll have you know I'm sort of seeing someone," Georgi stammered.

Nice, Petersen. Real smooth.

"Emil told me. Dirk the Dweeb."

She pursed her lips. "No one calls him that any more. He's senior vice president for commercial banking at the Spring Grove Savings & Loan."

"Emil also says you two aren't serious."

It was official. When Emil recovered, she was going to kill him.

"Emil talks too much." She snatched up her bag. "I knew this was a bad idea."

Jax uncrossed his superhero arms and took a step toward her. "What? Kissing me back?"

She countered, moving away from him. "I did not kiss you back."

"Liar." Undeterred, he closed in further, cupping her chin in his hand. He ran a thumb over her lips, caressing from one corner to the other and back again. "Do you kiss the Dweeb like that?"

"S … stop." Dammit, she was stammering again. She shook her head, breaking their contact. Not that that stopped her skin from tingling where he'd touched her. "You're not playing fair."

"I'm not playing."

"You promised." Perfect. She'd sunk to whining like a Kardashian over a little weight gain. She took a deep breath and started again, making a conscious effort to sound like a normal, rational adult. "Strictly business. That's the only way this is going to work."

"I'm sorry." He stuffed his hands in the pockets of his jeans and backed off, giving her some space. "You're right."

"I am?" She was. "I mean, I am."

Then why, as she watched him stride toward the stage calling Harvey's name, did she feel so alone all of a sudden?

It had been years since Jax had set foot in the Willoughby Wallace Memorial Library. Twelve years, to be exact.

He smiled as he remembered his last time there. In the stacks, with Georgi. His hand up her shirt, her mouth on his neck. She'd wanted to study, of course. He'd convinced her to take a not-so-short break for some play time.

"Jax Donovan. As I live and breathe."

"Mrs. Jensen." Some things never changed. The tiny, white-haired woman in her sweater sets and pince-nez glasses had been the reference librarian since dinosaurs roamed the earth. "As beautiful as ever."

"Aren't you the charmer? Still." She held out a palm. "And I believe you still owe us seven dollars in overdue fines."

"To Kill a Mockingbird." Georgi had insisted he read it before they watched the movie in their tenth grade English class instead of relying on the Cliff's Notes, like he usually did. He'd loved it so much he hadn't wanted to return it until she surprised him with his own copy. Dog-eared and cracked from multiple readings, it still had a place of honor on his bookshelf. "Worth every penny. I'll be sure to square up before I leave. But right now I'm due to read to a group of preschoolers."

"Ah, yes. The Book Buddies. They're expecting you. In the children's room, upstairs." She pointed him toward a spiral staircase.

"Georgi's still in the dark about who today's guest reader is, right?"

"Yep." She gave him a saucy wink. "It wasn't easy, but we kept it a surprise, just like you asked."

"Thanks, Mrs. Jenkins. I owe you one." He bussed her on the cheek and sprinted up the stairs.

"More like eight," she called after him. "If you count the overdue fines."

He smiled to himself as he reached the second floor and followed the sound of laughter down a short hallway to the children's room.

Phase two of Operation Get Georgie Back was underway.

The kiss had been a ploy. A way to find out if their old spark was still there. And boy, was it. More like a five-alarm fire. Now that he knew their passion hadn't faded any over the years, it was time for him to show her what had changed.

Him.

Show business had sobered him, matured him. He'd had his share of ups and downs along the way and learned how rare and truly valuable real friends – the kind who stuck with you through the downs –

were. Even more than a lover, Georgi had been his first real friend, the one who'd helped him through his parents' bitter divorce by introducing him to the fantasy world of the theater. And he'd thrown that away without a second thought in the way only a teenage boy brimming with hubris and self-importance could do.

Reading to the kids at the library was a brilliant idea to kick off this part of his plan, if he did say so himself. He did a lot of outreach with kids in New York: school visits, workshops, talk backs after performances. It was one of the best parts of his job. Usually the students were a little older than the preschool set, but it was never too young to introduce kids to theater, and he'd brought along one of his favorite books on the subject for youth, Thomas Schumacher's *How Does the Show Go On?*, to help.

Plus, it meant he could catch Georgi off guard, on different turf. He'd given her some breathing room in the three rehearsals they'd had since their kiss. Out of respect for her wishes, sure, but also because there was just too damn much to do in too short a time. He'd forgotten what it was like working with amateurs. Their enthusiasm was contagious, a welcome change from the attitude of many of the professional actors he worked with in New York, who'd become jaded thanks to endless auditions and countless rejections. But it seemed to take twice as long to get anything done.

Here, away from all that, he could concentrate on Georgi. And the twenty or so Book Buddies and associated parents he could see through the glassed-in door to the children's room, clustered on a brightly colored rug with the letters of the alphabet on it, waiting for their guest reader.

Jax braced for Georgi's reaction – would she be happy to see him? pissed off? knee him in the balls? – and pushed the door open.

"I hear the door, boys and girls. That must be our super-secret, special guest. Let's give a warm Book Buddies welcome to …" She turned to face the door and froze. "You."

He smiled and held his arms out, palms up. "Me."

He had to hand it to her. She recovered faster than a sacked quarterback, focusing her attention back on the kids. "This is Jax Donovan. He's a famous director on Broadway. Does anyone know where that is?"

"It's far, far away," a towheaded tot piped up. "Like in Ohio. Or outer space."

"You think everything is about space, Jared," another boy said, shooting the towhead a look of four-year-old disdain. "It's in New York City. There's singing and dancing and my dad says it's for girls."

A woman – clearly the second boy's mother – shushed him.

"Not every play has singing and dancing. And there's plenty of boys working on Broadway." Jax stepped in. "On stage and backstage."

"Are you an actor?"

"Do you have to kiss girls?"

"Do you like it?"

"Is it sloppy? My older sister says kissing is sloppy."

Jax fought hard not to laugh out loud at their precocious questions. They were an adorable bunch. Well, except for the one who thought Broadway was for girls. That kid needed a lesson in gender stereotyping. Or, better yet, his father.

"I was an actor," Jax said, deciding to answer the first question and hopefully skip the other three (yes, yes and not if it's done right). "But now I'm a director."

"What's that?"

"It means he gets to boss everyone around," the pint-sized sexist answered.

"Not exactly." Jax held up the Schumacher book. "But I brought this to help me explain it."

Georgi motioned for him to sit in a plastic chair barely big enough to accommodate one butt cheek. He balanced himself precariously, and for the next hour he tried to ignore the appraising glances some of the moms were throwing his way as he read and answered questions on everything from what "break a leg" meant to whether he knew Buzz Lightyear.

"That's all for today, kids." Georgi, who'd been lurking in the background, spoke up. "Say 'thank you' to Mr. Donovan for taking time out of his busy schedule to be with us."

"Thank you, Mr. Donovan," the kids chanted, running to their mothers or to the play area in the far corner of the room.

"Yes, thank you." The most obvious of the red hot mamas came up to him, offering her hand for him to shake. And, if her eyes weren't lying, a whole lot more if he gave her even the slightest encouragement.

He took her hand and shook it stiffly. "My pleasure."

Out of habit, he looked at her ring finger. Empty. A year ago – hell, a few months ago – he'd have taken her up on her clear invitation.

Not today. Not anymore. He was done with good-time girls. He wanted a forever girl. He wanted Georgi.

The woman in question appeared at his shoulder. "Serena, Mrs. Jenkins found that book you wanted.

It's downstairs at the main circulation desk."

"Great." She didn't even spare a glance for Georgi, her eyes remaining locked on Jax. "I can walk you out."

"I'll have to pass." He dropped her hand. "Georgi and I have some business to discuss. About the musical."

"That's right, I heard you were directing this year," Serena practically purred. "It's about time Emil stepped down."

"He did not step down," Georgi protested. "He passed out at the Stop 'n' Slurp."

"Whatever." Serena pulled a business card out of her wallet and handed it to Jax. "Call me if you need any help. I'm a cosmetologist. I could do hair and makeup."

"That's my stage manager's department. I'll pass this on to him." He shoved the card into the pocket of his jeans and addressed Georgi, effectively dismissing the other woman. He hoped. "Can we talk in your office?"

"Oh, we definitely have to talk." She stalked past him to a glass-enclosed office behind the children's circulation desk, calling to the younger woman at manning the desk as she passed. "Hold down the fort here, Stephanie. I need to speak to Mr. Donovan."

Ooooh. He was going to get spoken to. Why did that sound dirty to him? Why did everything out of her mouth sound dirty to him?

Jax trailed after Georgi, closing the office door behind him.

She didn't waste any time digging right into him. "What the hell are you doing here?"

"I would have thought that was obvious. Reading to the kids."

"You know what I mean." She crossed to a wall of bookshelves, putting the large, oak desk as a barrier between them. "This is my place of business, Jax."

"This wasn't about you, Georgi." Okay, so it was. Partially. But she didn't have to know that. "I do a lot of theater education in New York. I figured I might as well do some of the same while I'm here."

She sank into the desk chair. "I didn't know that."

He sat on the corner of the desk, resisting the urge to lean across it and breathe her in. He knew exactly how she'd smell. Delicate and floral and alluring. "There's a lot you don't know about me, Georgi."

"Apparently."

"Look, can we call a truce?" He gave her his patented puppy dog face. "I've been a good boy. No more fooling around at rehearsals. And I had the best intentions here. Cut me some slack."

She tilted her head to study him. "We'll see."

"We'll see?"

"That's all you're going to get for now." She pushed the chair away from the desk, stood and went to the door. "I have work to do. And you, sir, have a show to direct. Shouldn't you be gathering props or painting sets or something?"

"Fine. I'll go. But I'll be back this afternoon."

She opened the door and held it for him. "This afternoon?"

He hopped off the desk and crossed to her. "Who

do you think's your surprise guest for the six-to-eight-year-old Reading Rangers?"

Three

"You're looking a thousand times better." Georgi handed Emil a cup of tea and tucked his blanket around his legs.

"I wish people would stop treating me like a goddamn invalid." He sipped the tea and grimaced. "And I wish the doc would let me have something stronger than tea. You wouldn't consider spiking it with of a little of the brandy I've got stashed in the cabinet above the refrigerator, would you?"

"No, I wouldn't." Georgi smiled in spite of herself. Emil made it hard to hate him, even when he was meddling in her love life. "I'm mad at you, remember?"

"You won't let me forget." He took another sip of tea, grimaced again and set the cup down on the coffee table. "Are you ever going to forgive me for bringing Jax here?"

She sat on the end of the couch. "I don't know. Are you ever going to tell me why you did it?"

"I couldn't think of anyone else qualified to replace me."

"Try again."

"His latest show just closed and I figured he'd be at loose ends."

"Strike two."

"I confess. I thought having Jax around might help you realize you're settling with that boring banker. So sue me."

"Now we're getting somewhere." Georgi leaned

back and crossed her legs. "Dirk is not boring. And he's here, not off in New York City."

"Pretty low standards, if you asked me."

"And, most importantly, he's never broken my heart."

"That again?" Emil clucked his tongue. "Georgi Girl, in the words of that new American musical classic *Frozen*, you need to let it go."

"Let it go?" she shrieked, bristling inside at the nickname only he and Jax had ever called her. "He bailed on me, on all our plans, and his idea of a goodbye was a three-line note that he stuck under the windshield wiper of my car in the Caron's Corner parking lot."

"Have you ever given him the chance to explain why he left the way he did?"

She shifted uncomfortably in her seat. "Well, not exactly."

"What sort of an answer is that?" Emil frowned. "It's a simple question. Either you did or you didn't."

"Okay, I didn't," she admitted.

"Then don't you think it's high time you did?"

"Have you talked to Jax?" Georgi asked, suddenly suspicious. "Do you know something I don't know?"

"Of course I've talked to him. He comes to see me almost every day. But I don't know what you know, so how can I know if I know more than you?"

She rolled her eyes. "I won't even pretend to have followed that."

"Besides, whatever you need to hear needs to come from him."

"I don't need to hear anything from him."

"Yes, you do. Whether it's to rekindle the old flame or to get closure." Emil waggled his eyebrows at her. The feisty devil was clearly on the mend. "Personally, I'm voting for rekindle the old flame."

"So noted." Georgi pulled out her phone and swiped the screen. "It's almost time for dinner. I brought you something special."

"If it's not chicken soup, scrambled eggs or tofu – whatever the hell that is – I'll be happy."

She stood, relieved that Emil had gone along with

her change in topic so easily. Probably because he was hitting a little too close to home. Was he right? Should she have given Jax a chance to explain all those years ago? He'd certainly tried in the weeks after his abrupt departure. Phone calls. Texts. Emails. All of which she'd ignored or deleted without opening. She'd been young and immature, too consumed with hurt to listen to what he had to say.

Was she ready now?

She'd have to do some serious thinking about that. Later. Right now, she had a cranky, hungry patient to deal with. "None of the above. But it is doctor approved for your budding ulcer. I'll go heat it up. We can eat together before I go to rehearsal."

"Good. I want to hear all about how things are going. Did Sebastian learn his lines yet? How's the set looking? Has Janine finished choreographing the eleventh hour number?"

"Patience, grasshopper," Georgi tossed over her shoulder as she headed through the swinging door into the kitchen. "All will be revealed. In time."

She pulled the vegetable casserole she'd brought out of the fridge, made up a plate and stuck it in the microwave, setting the timer for three minutes. She watched, transfixed, as it spun around and around on the turntable. Was this what she was destined for? Microwave meals for one? Having friends come over and wait on her in her dotage?

She assembled a second plate and hunted through the cabinets and drawers for utensils and napkins. The microwave dinged, and she swapped the plates. When it dinged a second time, she gathered plates, utensils and napkins and brought it all out to the living room.

"Is you tea cold?" she asked as she laid everything out on the coffee table. "I could heat it up for you if you like."

"Don't bother," Emil grumbled. "Hot or cold, it still tastes like ass."

She chuckled and helped him sit up so he could eat. "What, pray tell, does ass taste like?"

"You're an actress." He lifted a forkful of casserole to his mouth. "Use your imagination."

"Well, I think you'll at least enjoy dinner. I even managed to sneak in a little pepper."

"Salt?" he asked hopefully.

She shook her head and loaded her own fork with casserole. "Sorry, no can do. Doc's worried about your blood pressure."

"My blood pressure, my cholesterol, my prostate. That man will worry about anything."

"He's your doctor. It's his job."

They dug in, alternating conversation with bites of casserole. They weren't five minutes into the meal when her cell rang. She pulled it out of her pocket and checked the screen.

"It's Jax." He'd had the whole cast program his number into their phones in case they needed to reach him in an emergency, which even she had to admit was pretty generous for a bigwig like him. "I hope nothing's wrong."

"Only one way to find out," Emil said through a mouthful of casserole. "Answer it."

She pressed "accept" and put the phone to her ear.

"Hello?"

"Georgi, it's Jax. We've got a slight problem with rehearsal tonight."

Crap. Time was running short. They really couldn't afford to lose a minute in the theater.

"What's wrong?"

"Sebastian is sick."

"How sick?" The guy was a hypochondriac. He probably had a little sniffle. She'd go over to his place, tell him to suck it up and drag him to rehearsal if she had to.

"Sinus infection. He'll be out three days, minimum."

Double crap.

"What about his understudy?"

"Harvey said he quit a month ago and they never bothered to replace him. Job transfer to the west coast."

Triple crap. She'd forgotten about that.

"The good news is Sebastian will be back by tech week," Jax continued. "But we've got three rehearsals before then."

"Without an understudy, what can we do?" She glanced over at Emil, who was avidly following her end of the conversation while continuing to shovel food into his mouth. You'd think the man hadn't eaten in a week.

"I have an idea." Jax paused so long Georgi thought the call had dropped until he finally spoke again. "But I'm not sure you'll like it."

"Try me."

"There is one person who knows this play and every part in it like the back of his hand."

Oh, sweet baby cheesus. She could see where this was going.

"Harvey?" she asked, knowing her answer was dead wrong. Their stage manager preferred to stay behind the scenes, out of the spotlight.

"Stage fright," Jax answered, confirming her suspicions.

"You?" She shot a panicked look at Emil.

"Bingo. But if it'll make you uncomfortable …"

She wasn't sure uncomfortable was the right word. It would make her … something. But as Jax had reminded her when he'd visited the library, not everything was about her. She had the whole cast and crew to consider. Without those rehearsals, the likelihood of the show opening on schedule – or at all – was next to nil.

"If it makes it any better, I promise to stay on my best behavior." Jax sounded like an eager puppy. "Strictly business, like we agreed."

"What about the love scenes?" She and Sebastian had no less than three hot and heavy smooches. She'd never make it through them playing opposite Jax without creaming her panties.

"We can skip 'em. Mark 'em. Do 'em as written. Whichever you prefer."

"Okay."

"Okay what?"

"Okay, I'm in. We can feel our way through the love scenes."

"Feel our way?" A hint of playfulness crept into

his voice. "Sounds like fun."

Damn. She'd walked right into that one. "It's a figure of speech."

"Best behavior. Scout's honor. See you at rehearsal in an hour."

He ended the call and she sat staring for a moment at her phone.

"Let me guess." Emil's face was split into a shit-eating grin. "From the half of the conversation I could hear, I'd say Sebastian's out and Jax is taking his place."

"You don't have to look so happy about it." She picked up her plate, keeping an eye on the clock to make sure she had enough time to finish dinner and get to the theater.

"It's beyond my wildest expectations."

"Before you get too satisfied with yourself and all your scheming, you should know it's only for a few days. Sebastian will be back on his feet for tech week."

"No matter." Emil waved a hand and smiled

impossibly wider, his watery, whiskey-brown eyes sporting a twinkle that had been missing as of late with his illness. "Sometimes a few days is all it takes for two stubborn idiots to come to their senses and realize they're still in love with each other."

Jax was on his second Hungry Man dinner of the night – what the hell kind of hungry man subsisted on a couple of slivers of Salisbury steak, a glob of mashed potatoes and a handful of string beans? – when the doorbell rang.

He paused the DVD he'd been watching. *The Music Man*, his senior show at Spring Grove High School. Him as the title character, Georgi as his leading lady, Marian the librarian. Funny how the show had been prophetic in some ways. And not in others.

Being on stage with her again this week had been like riding a bicycle. It had all come rushing back to him. The way they read each other's emotions, anticipated each other's movements. Their chemistry on stage was as strong as ever.

Off stage, too, if he could just get her to admit it.

The bell chimed again, bringing him back from his mental journey to the past. He padded in bare feet across the tiny living room of the short-term rental Abner had set up for him and cracked open the door.

"I brought baklava."

Georgi stood on the stoop, a plastic wrapped tray in her outstretched arms.

"Shouldn't you save it for rehearsal? The cast loves sweets."

She bit her lip and looked down at the tray. "I needed to talk to you alone. The baklava is because my mom taught me never to show up at someone's house empty-handed."

"Is something wrong?"

"Not exactly. Can I come in?"

"Oh, sure." *Inconsiderate asshole.* He stepped back and held the door open. "Sorry."

She breezed past him and put the tray down on the

coffee table.

He shut the door and leaned against it. "Can I get you something to drink? Water? Juice? Some of that throat coat tea you like?"

"You noticed."

"Of course I noticed. I notice everything about you."

"You know who else does that?"

"Who?"

"Stalkers."

"Very funny." He pushed off the door and stuffed his hands in his pockets. "Tell you what. Grab that tray, follow me into the kitchen, and I'll make us both some tea. Then we can talk."

"How about a glass of wine instead?"

"Wine it is."

She picked up the baklava and trailed after him. "So this is where Abner set you up."

He shrugged and pulled a couple of wine glasses down from the cabinet next to the sink. "It's not the Ritz, but it'll do. Red or white?"

He held up a bottle in each hand.

"White, thanks."

He motioned for her to sit at the butcher block, poured them each a glass and joined her.

"Baklava?" She uncovered the tray and pushed it across to him.

"Thanks." He took one piece of the sticky-sweet treat and bit into it. "Did you make this?"

"Guilty as charged." An adorable flush crept up her cheeks. "Learning to make baklava is a rite of passage in every Greek household."

"It's delicious. Now quit stalling and tell me what's bothering you."

She sipped her wine. "Who said anything was bothering me?"

"You. Coming to see me. At night. Alone."

She stalled again, nibbling on a piece of baklava, and he could see that, whatever it was she wanted to get off her chest, it wasn't easy for her.

Maybe a little game of twenty questions would lighten things up.

"Is it about Sebastian?" Her co-star was due back tomorrow. Not something Jax was looking forward to.

She shook her head.

"Something else to do with the show?"

Another head shake.

"Us?"

Finally. A nod. Too bad it was in response to the one question where he really, really wanted a shake.

"I've been a good boy, haven't I? Practically a saint."

"Yes, you have. It's not that." She licked a few crumbs of the flaky baklava off her lips.

Jax fought to ignore the tightening in his trousers and took her hand across the butcher block. "Spit it out. Fast. Like ripping off a Band-Aid."

"I'm sorry for how I've been treating you." Once she started, the words tumbled out like chorus girls from an oversized cake. "And for not letting you explain why you left. I was a scared, hurt, dumb kid, and I've been holding to those feelings for years. It's time to let them go."

Jax pulled his hand back. "So you can be with someone else? Like Dirk?"

He wanted to swallow his damn jealous words the minute they were out of his mouth.

She shook her head. "I don't know."

"Come with me." He stood and offered her his hand, anxious to make up for his faux pas. She was finally ready to put the past behind them. He couldn't fuck this up now. "There's something I want to show you."

"Your etchings?" she joked.

"In a manner of speaking."

She took his hand and he led her back into the living room. They sat side by side on the sofa, and he picked up the remote for the DVD.

"Please tell me you're not making me watch porn." She gave him a sly smile. "Cause I gotta say, been there, done that, like it better live and in person."

"Really?" He quirked a brow at her. "I never took you for a voyeur."

She blushed even redder than before. "Doing it, I mean. Not watching."

"Good to know." He chuckled and pressed play. "And I couldn't agree more."

As luck would have it, the scene where he'd paused earlier was the one where he and Georgi – as Harold Hill and Marian Paroo – confessed their love for each other. In song, of course. He watched as his on-screen doppelganger moved in for the big clinch at the end of the number.

He remembered exactly how he'd felt at that instant. Not nervous but totally in the moment, immersed in his character. And in her.

"Oh. My. God." Georgi's pretty lips were parted in astonishment. "Where did you get this?"

"Where else? Emil. He has all our shows on DVD. *Grease. Kiss Me Kate. West Side Story.*"

"All that body makeup for *West Side Story*." She shuddered at the memory.

"Not me." He gave her a playful nudge with his elbow. "I played the pale-skinned Polish guy, remember?"

"God, look at you." She waved at the screen. "You're so good. And I'm so … awkward. No wonder NYU accepted you and not me."

"That's not what I see."

"Enlighten me."

He stared at the TV. "I see a girl who knew how to love with all her heart. And a boy too stupid to realize what he had."

"What did he have?" she asked breathlessly.

He turned to face her, snaking an arm across the back of the couch, dangerously close to her shoulders. "The love of his life."

"Then why did you leave the way you did? That note …"

The note. His stomach clenched when he thought of it. Three lines. A world of hurt.

"I thought … I don't know what I thought. That the distance would kill our relationship and we'd break up eventually. That it would hurt less if I ended it myself, fast."

"Like ripping off a Band-Aid?" she asked, echoing his advice to her in the kitchen.

"Something like that." Except it hadn't been as easy to cut her out of his life as he thought. Hence the string of phone calls, texts and emails, all of which had gone unanswered.

"Well, we'll never know whether we would have made it or not." She shifted almost imperceptibly away from him. "Because you never gave us the chance."

"You're right. And I know you don't owe me that courtesy now. But that's what I'm asking you for. A second chance."

"Why now?" She looked up at him, her eyes murky with confusion and something he hoped was – well, hope. "Why me?"

"Because, Georgi Girl." He closed in on her, trapping her between his body and the arm of the couch and cupping her face in his hands. "I'm not the kind of guy who repeats his mistakes. You're the one for me. I lost you once thanks to my own stupidity.

But I'm a hell of a lot smarter now, and I've got no intention of losing you again."

Four

Georgi was exactly where she wanted to be. Her face in Jax's warm, strong hands. Her breasts crushed against his muscular chest. Her heart beating a million times a minute as he shifted impossibly closer so his thigh pressed into hers.

And still something held her back.

"I'm … the one?" She wanted to believe him. Really, she did. He sounded so sure. But it had been so long since they'd been together. How could he know?

"I won't lie to you, Georgi." He pulled back slightly and met her gaze full on. "I'm no angel. I've been with my fair share of women. But none of them understood me like you. None of them supported me like you. None of them made my breath catch and my pulse pound and my palms sweat like you."

"Sounds serious." She tilted her head to study him. "Maybe you should see a doctor for that."

"I don't need a doctor." He caressed her cheek with his thumb, creating a jolt of electricity that radiated all the way down to her toes, which she wiggled in her sandals. "You're the cause. And the cure."

"How many of your women have you used that line on?"

"None." His hands slipped down to her shoulders. "I told you, Georgi. You're different. I'm different with you. I want that."

"For how long?"

"As long as you'll have me."

"I've got roots here in Spring Grove. Your work is mostly in New York. How …?"

"We're on the same coast, not across the world. We'll figure things out if we want it bad enough." His grip on her shoulders tightened. "I do. Do you?"

She thought about her parents and how in love they'd been. She thought about Emil, alone in front of his television. She thought about Dirk the Dweeb and how, nice as he was, he never gave her the breath-catching, pulse-pounding, palms-sweating feeling she apparently inspired in Jax. The feeling he inspired in her.

"Yes," she said finally, her voice almost a whisper. "I do."

"Thank God," he muttered in the second before his lips swooped down to capture hers. A low, sexy groan rumbled up from deep in his throat and his tongue swept the seam of her mouth, coaxing her to open to him.

And open she did, meeting his tongue with hers, tasting him. Sweet wine and sweeter baklava. She'd been starving for this, for him, and now that she'd had a sample she wasn't stopping until she'd gorged herself.

Her body rocked into his, her nipples hardening into points and practically boring through the thin material of her blouse. With a groan of pleasure, he pulled the offending garment from the waistband of her shorts and inched it up her rib cage, his fingers brushing the undersides of her breasts through her satin bra.

"Hands up," he ordered, breaking the kiss.

She'd never been one to take orders, but when he bossed her around in that smoky, sexy voice of his she was helpless to resist. Her hands shot up and he lifted her shirt over her head, tossing it onto the floor.

"Damn." He cupped her silk-clad breasts in his hands. "You grew up nice."

Georgi swallowed hard as Jax's eyes raked up and down her nearly naked torso, sending sparks to all her girly zones. She slid her hands under his T-shirt and ran them over his washboard abs and solid pecs. His skin was hot under her palms. "So did you."

He leaned in closer, his mouth hovering by one ear. "You were hot when you came. I bet you're even hotter now."

Her eyes drifted closed and she bit her lip. "I bet the sex is hotter, too."

"Shall we test that theory?" He nipped her earlobe then licked the tinge of pain away.

"Yes, please." She whimpered as his lips traveled down her neck to the hollow at the base of her throat.

"It might take all night."

She opened her eyes and looked into his, dark and heavy lidded with desire. And something more. Need. For her. She shuddered with an answering need. "I don't have anywhere else to go."

"I do." Without warning, Jax scooped her up and carried her upstairs. "The bedroom."

Georgi wrapped her arms around his neck and held on tight. She could feel his heart beating as fast as hers through the cotton of his T-shirt as he reached the top of the stairs and started down the hall.

"Here we are." He kicked the door open and deposited her on the bed. "Not as big as the king at my place in New York, but I'm sure we'll find a way to make do."

She felt a momentary pang at his mention of New York, but it disappeared when he shucked his shirt, revealing the hills and valleys of his ripped pecs and abs, and stretched out on the bed next to her.

"How do you do it?"

"Do what?"

"Look like … that." She waved her hand up and down his torso. "I thought directors were supposed to be middle-aged, bald and paunchy."

"Nope, nope and nope. I'm no gym rat, but there's a facility in my building and I work out a few times a week. Directing is more physical than it looks. It's not all taking notes and drinking coffee. I have to stay in shape to keep up with my actors." He eyed her denim cutoffs. "But enough about me. I want to focus on you. More specifically, getting you out of those shorts."

"I can help with that." She kicked off her sandals and raised her hips.

He took up the invitation and reached for her waistband, slowly pulling her shorts down over her hips, thighs, calves, ankles and finally feet, his fingers brushing her skin as he went and leaving a trail of goosebumps in their wake.

She laid back and looked up at him, saying a silent prayer of thanks that she'd had the foresight to put on a matching set of bra and panties that morning. And not only matching, one of her best sets, purple satin from La Perla. Was it luck, or was she secretly hoping this would happen when she got dressed, knowing she planned to go to him that night?

"Now you." She fingered his belt buckle.

"I can help with that," he said, parroting her words.

He stood, making it easier for him to unbuckle his belt, release his jeans, slide them down his long, powerful legs and kick them to one side.

"No underwear?" she asked, staring at his naked form. Jesus, Mary and Joseph on a bicycle, the man was beautiful. Like an Italian Renaissance statue in dark-rimmed glasses, which he used that moment to remove and place on the bedside table.

"I like the boys to swing free."

She licked her lips. "So do I."

He laughed deep in his throat and it traveled through her like a lightning bolt of lust as he rejoined her on the bed and stroked his fingertips along her body.

"I want to taste you," he said, his voice a sexy growl. "Everywhere."

"Yes," she breathed.

"Should I start here?" He fastened his mouth around one nipple, sucked and withdrew, leaving a damp patch of silk where his lips had been.

"Or here?" He did the same to her other nipple, making her arch into him.

"Or maybe I should dive right into the main course." He trailed moist kisses down her body, ending at the patch of silk covering her sex. His warm, wet breath teased her through the filmy fabric.

"Here."

"Jax, please." She let her legs fall open wider.

"Okay." He slipped his thumbs under the waistband of her panties and tugged downward. "Main course it is, then."

He had Georgi. In his bed. Naked.

Or she would be once he got her bra and panties off.

Her skin was as soft as the silk of her skivvies as he drew them down her long, slim legs and over her ankles and feet. He tossed the panties aside and turned his attention back to her pretty, pink-tipped toes, massaging first them then her arches and heels.

"Jax," she moaned. "You promised."

"Promised what?" He moved up past her ankles to her calves.

"You said you wanted to … taste me." She blushed furiously.

"And taste you I shall." He planted a kiss behind

one knee. Christ, he loved teasing her, seeing the color rush to her cheeks. "In good time. We have all night, remember?"

"Not if I die of anticipation," she quipped.

"We can't have that, can we?" He laughed against her thigh as he worked his way oh-so-slowly to the place she wanted him.

She was squirming underneath him by the time he parted her folds with his fingers and touched his tongue to her clit. She jerked against him like he'd touched her with a live wire.

Always so responsive, his Georgi Girl.

"Yes," she panted, gasping as if she couldn't get enough air.

But it was him who couldn't get enough. Of her touch, her taste, her sweet essence. He added a finger to the mix, thrusting it inside her, and she jerked again, nearly coming off the bed.

"You always liked that, didn't you?" he asked, angling his finger to hit that perfect spot, the one that always made her come apart.

"God, yes." She reached down to thread a hand through his hair, keeping him right where she wanted him as he continued to swirl his tongue and pump one finger, then two.

Every muscle in her body was on edge, tensing and twitching, so close to orgasm. He'd seen her like this enough to know. And he wanted to see it again.

"Come for me," her groaned against her mound.

"So close." She pulled tight against him, reaching for her release. The fingers in his hair dug into his scalp.

"That's right, baby. Just like that."

One spasm, two, three and she shattered underneath him. He pulled his fingers free and lifted his head, her juices dampening his face, her scent – musky and erotic – surrounding him.

"That was … wow." She disentangled her hand from his hair, coming away with a few strands trapped between her fingers. "Oops. Sorry."

"I'm not." He slid up her body, coming to rest with his dick nestled between her legs, rubbing against her still warm, still wet center. "A willing sacrifice for the cause."

"The cause?"

"Your satisfaction."

She arched into him. "And what about your satisfaction?"

"We're getting to that, sweetheart." He met her movements with his own, making him harder and her wetter. "We're getting to that."

"I want you to ... get there." She buried her face in the crook of his shoulder so he couldn't see the color he was pretty sure was flooding her cheeks. "But I'm not sure I can ... get there ... again."

"Are you kidding?" He snaked a finger under her chin, tilting it up and forcing her to look at him. "Do you remember senior prom? I think you came five times."

"Six, actually." There was the blush he knew and loved. "But who was counting?"

"So what's the problem?"

She averted her eyes. "The problem is I haven't had

a multiple orgasm since."

"Seriously?"

"I know. I'm a freak and you probably want to run as far away from me as possible." She tried to squirm out from underneath him.

"Are you kidding?" He trapped her between the mattress and his body. "Do you know how it makes me feel, knowing I'm the only man who can make you come, and come, and come, and …?"

"You're getting a little ahead of yourself, aren't you, hot shot?" She reached up to caress his face.

"You're right. Time to put my dick where my mouth is." He turned his head to kiss her palm. "Or was."

He twisted sideways to rummage through the nightstand for a condom. Ripping open the packet and rolling it on, he entered her in one long, slow thrust, knowing if he took her hard and fast, like his cock was screaming for him to do, it would be over all too soon. She clenched around him, hot and tight, digging her nails into his shoulders, his back, his hips. He'd be a marked man tomorrow, that was for sure. Not that he was complaining.

This was Georgi. His Georgi. As familiar as his favorite pair of Converse. Sex with her had never been boring, sometimes been challenging and always been stimulating.

"Wrap your legs around me," he urged.

She complied, locking her ankles behind his back and allowing him to thrust even deeper. Long, languorous thrusts designed to bring them both to the crest and over, slipping, sliding, falling together.

He slithered a hand between them to cup her breast, pushing down the satiny cup of her bra and flicking the nipple with his thumb. He pulled almost all the way out of her and she moaned in protest before he pushed back in, hard enough so her breasts jiggled and her heels dug into his back. She lifted her hips to meet him, pushing when he pulled, pulling when he pushed, the two of them working together in perfect, torturous rhythm.

"I'm not …" She sucked in a breath as he almost

withdrew again, only to come back even harder, deeper. "I can't."

"You are." He ducked his head to nip her neck. He wouldn't be the only one with marks in the morning. "And you can."

"Jax," she groaned, her hands clutching at his shoulders.

"Come on." He sped up the rhythm. "Let go with me."

"Yes."

"Ready?"

"Almost."

"There."

He felt her come apart again around him, and then he was following her, shuddering his own release while he whispered her name.

She sank back onto the bed with an exhausted sigh and he collapsed next to her.

"Two down," she murmured into his chest. "Four to go."

He reached between them and held her hand,

smiling as he twined his fingers with hers. He hadn't thought it was possible, but she was right.

The sex was hotter.

Five

"Five minutes to curtain, everyone," Harvey called backstage. "Five minutes."

"Thank you, five," Georgi chorused along with the rest of the cast.

"And Mr. Donovan wants to see everyone in the green room, stat."

Georgi put the finishing touches on her makeup and made her way to the green room, humming to herself as she went. It was amazing how things could change in just a few weeks.

She and Jax had spent every night together since she'd visited him bearing baklava. They made dinner, made plans, made love. Neither one of them had said the three magic words yet, but she had a feeling it was just a matter of time.

And the theater, which had been on the verge of shutting its doors? Well, if everything went as planned tonight, the investors Jax had lured up from New York would have the money flowing in and the construction crews at work before the month was out.

She opened the door of the green room to find most of the cast already gathered around Jax.

"Ah, here's our star." He waved her into the room. "Now that we're all here, I'd like to say a few words before you take the stage tonight."

He paused and scanned the crowd, his eyes lighting an almost undetectable moment longer on Georgi. "It's been an honor and a privilege for me to step into Emil's shoes and direct this fine company.

You've helped me to rediscover the joy of performing for the pure love of it, of telling a story and sharing it with the audience, without all the commercialization of professional theater. When I go back to New York, it will be with a renewed spirit and sense of excitement, and that's because of you all. For that, I am eternally grateful."

The cast burst into applause, which Jax quickly quieted. "Now, I want you to go out there tonight and hold nothing back. Commit fully, leave it all on the stage. And most importantly, have fun."

"Are the investors here?" one of the ensemble members asked.

"Are we going to be able to save the theater?" another chimed in.

"Yes, the investors are here. But I don't want any of you to be worrying about them tonight," Jax answered. "Remember, when you're acting, none of this …" He waved an arm around the room. "Exists. You're in a different place, a different time. Stay focused."

"Places, everyone," Harvey announced. "Places."

With hugs and kisses galore and many a chant of "break a leg" – theater speak for good luck – the cast dispersed. Before Georgi could follow them to take her starting position stage left, Jax caught her arm, holding her back.

"I want you to know," he said, his mouth close to her ear and his voice low so only she could hear, "no matter what happens tonight, I'm committed to you and this theater."

No matter what happens tonight? That sounded ominous.

But she didn't have time to dwell on it. With a quick kiss, Jax released her and gave her a gentle shove toward the door.

"Go," he said. "Be brilliant."

"Thanks." She blew him a kiss and ducked out of the room.

A little under three hours and four curtain calls later, Georgi just about flew off the stage.

"Great job, Georgi."

"Yeah, you were awesome."

"As always."

Georgi acknowledged and returned all the congratulatory words on her way to her dressing room. Once inside, she shut the door and slumped against it, happy for a moment of quiet. She closed her eyes and let the familiar feelings wash over her – exhilaration, pride, camaraderie, relief. And with them, something new. The knowledge that she had someone to share them with.

She crossed the room to sit at her dressing table, shucking off her character shoes and reaching for a baby wipe to remove her stage makeup. She'd barely started when she heard a knock at the door.

"You decent?" Jax's voice floated through the closed door.

"Unfortunately." She grabbed another wipe. "Come in."

He entered the room, three bouquets of flowers in his arms.

"This one's from the staff at the library," he said

placing a yellow and orange arrangement on her dressing table. "And this one's from Emil."

He added a small bouquet of pink tulips to the pile. "And this one …"

He held out a stunning assortment of roses in all the colors of the rainbow. "This one is from me. You were fabulous. You even made Sebastian look good. Just don't tell him I said so."

"Thanks." She took it and buried her nose in the blooms, inhaling deeply. Their sweet smell filled her nostrils. "They're beautiful."

"Not as beautiful as you." He dropped a kiss on her forehead. "Now get changed so we can get to the cast party."

"Do we have to?" She pouted, anxious to get him alone. She only had him full-time for a few more days before he went back to New York, and she intended to make the most of every second.

"Yes, we have to." He took his flowers from her and laid them on top of the others. "But the sooner we get there, the sooner we can leave."

She turned back to the mirror above her dressing table and pulled a fresh wipe from the container. "Sounds like my kind of plan."

The party was at the Kettle. They'd set out a buffet of the cast's favorites: hot wings, loaded potato skins, fried mozzarella. Georgie grabbed a drink from the bar and mingled while Jax huddled with two of his investor friends in a corner. After about half an hour, he emerged with his arms around them and a broad smile on his face.

"Can I have your attention please?" he asked when they reached the center of the room. He caught Georgi's eye and winked, maybe remembering that he'd uttered the same line as conman Harold Hill and wound up with a whole town under his spell. Kind of like how Spring Grove was under his spell now. "These two gentlemen are with the Churchill Foundation in New York. And I'm happy to announce that they've agreed to provide the funds necessary for the theater's renovation."

A cheer rose up from the crowd.

"So everyone, please, eat, drink and celebrate your hard work knowing that this is not the end for the arts in Spring Grove."

The cast and crew swarmed him then, shaking his hand, clapping him on the back, thanking his friends from the Churchill Foundation. Georgi hung back, knowing she'd have her chance later. They'd been discrete about their relationship so far, not wanting it to interfere with the cast dynamic. They'd go public soon, but until then she was content to stay in the shadows.

"Georgi." A familiar voice came from behind her shoulder. "Great show tonight."

"Thanks, Dirk." She turned to face him. "How have you been?"

"Fine, thanks." He scuffed at the carpet with his loafer and stuffed his hands in his pockets. "A little lonely since you turned me down the last three times I asked you out."

"I'm sorry, Dirk. It's just that …" She hesitated, not sure how much to tell him. She opted for partial honesty as the best policy. "I'm sort of seeing someone."

"Sort of?"

She couldn't stop her eyes from flicking to Jax, still surrounded by well-wishers in the middle of the room. "It's not exactly official yet."

"Don't tell me you've fallen for our hometown hero?" Dirk pressed his lips into a thin line.

Dammit. The man might still be a bit of a dweeb, but she should have known he was way too sharp to miss the obvious signals she couldn't help but give off, like pheromones or something. When it came to hiding her emotions she was hopelessly horrible.

"I'm sorry," she said again, simply.

"Didn't you guys used to date in high school?" Dirk asked.

"Yes." She glanced around for an easy escape, desperate to get out of a conversation that was becoming more uncomfortable by the second. But everyone was otherwise occupied, either eating or drinking or dancing on the tiny parquet floor now that the DJ had started spinning tunes.

"So are you moving to England with him or is this going to be a long, long distance kind of thing?"

"What do you mean, England?" She turned back to Dirk, her forehead a wrinkled mass of confusion. What did England have to do with anything?

"You haven't heard? Your new boyfriend's going to be the next artistic director of the Royal Shakespeare Company. In London."

"That's … that's not true." It couldn't be true. He couldn't be doing this to her, running off and making decisions about their future without even consulting her. Again. Only this time he was running all the way to another continent.

Was that what he meant by "whatever happens tonight?"

"It was in *Variety* this morning," Dirk explained.

She frowned at him. "You read the trades?"

"No." Dirk rolled his eyes at the very thought of him picking up such a publication. "But when I heard you'd be working with Jax, I set a Google alert for him."

Stalker much?

"Why would you do that?"

"It's like Sun Tsu said. Know thy enemy."

"Jax is not your enemy."

"Maybe not. But if he's moving to another continent without even telling you, he might be yours." He pressed a few buttons on his phone and handed it to her. "Here. See for yourself."

He'd called up the *Variety* article. She only had to read the headline to know the story: "Broadway Director Jax Donovan Tapped for Top Job at RSC."

She thrust the phone at Dirk. "I … I have to go."

"I'm sorry to be the bearer of bad news." His self-satisfied smirk told another story.

"I'm sure you are." She fumbled for her purse, which she'd left hanging over the back of a nearby chair, and ran for the door, not knowing or caring who she pushed aside on her way to her escape. She was suffocating, the air closing in around her, her breath coming in short, sharp pants.

Jax Donovan had broken her heart again. And she'd let him.

What the hell had gone wrong?

One minute he was celebrating, complete with back-slapping and first-bumping, and the next he was chasing Georgi out of the restaurant, watching her get in her car and drive away in tears.

He'd asked around to try to find out what had sent her flying out of there. But all he could get was that she'd been talking to Dirk the Dweeb right before she left. And the Dweeb had taken off right after her, although his exit had been more stealthy than dramatic.

Damn, damn, damn, damn, damn.

Jax sat on the front steps of the restaurant and pulled out his cell phone to call her. He was surprised to find a whole host of new text messages. *Shit.* He'd turned the ringer off, not wanting to be disturbed before the show, and forgotten to turn it back on. He scrolled through them now, becoming more confused with each one.

Congrats, man.

Royal Shakespeare, that's huge.

Merry Old England is lucky to have you.

There were almost a hundred more texts in the same vein from people he'd worked with in one capacity or another: actors, techies, producers, fellow directors. Each one offering congratulations of some sort and mentioning England or the RSC.

He checked the time on the screen. Almost midnight. Too late to call his agent. But not too late to Google.

It only took a few clicks and swipes and he had the answer. Not that he liked it.

"What the fuck?" Someone had loose lips. And misinformation.

"Something wrong, son?" Emil sat on the step next to him and clapped a hand on his shoulder.

"Shouldn't you be in bed by now?" Jax eyeballed him, looking for any sign of illness or exhaustion.

"Does Doc Wolfson know you're out this late?"

"He gave me a get out of jail free card for tonight." Emil held up a half-eaten appetizer. "Even said I could have a wing or two."

"Are you sure that's smart?"

"Are you sure it was smart letting Georgi run off like that?"

"I didn't exactly let her run off."

"Any idea what got her knickers in a twist?"

"Yeah." Jax clicked back onto the *Variety* article handed Emil his cell phone. "This."

Emil read in silence for a minute, then looked up. "Is it true?"

"Of course it's not true." Jax ran a hand through his hair. "We had some discussions. Months ago. But nothing was settled, on their end or mine."

"But Georgi saw this and thinks it's a done deal."

"I assume."

"And you never said anything to her about it."

"Bingo."

"So now she thinks she's right back where she was

twelve years ago."

Crap. He hadn't thought about it that way. But it made sense she would.

"Wait, how did you know we are … were … seeing each other again? It's not like we took out a classified ad."

Emil shrugged and returned Jax's phone to him. "You visit me. She visits me. I've known you both since you were in braces. I can tell."

Crafty old codger. And they thought they'd been so smart visiting separately.

Jax punched Georgi's number into his cell.

Straight to voicemail.

"Dammit." He shoved the phone back in his pocket and buried his head in his hands. "How am I supposed to explain if she won't take my calls? It's like deja vu all over again."

"Then make sure history doesn't repeat itself." Emil slapped him on the back. "Make her hear you. Follow her to the ends of the earth if necessary."

"It won't be necessary."

A soft voice made him raise his head. "Georgi. You came back."

"I came back."

"And that's my cue to leave." Emil stood and gave Georgi a peck on the cheek. "You were wonderful tonight, Georgi Girl."

He leaned in and whispered in her ear, but not so softly that Jax couldn't catch what he was saying. "Listen to him."

With a wink and a jaunty whistle, Emil disappeared back into the restaurant.

"I didn't hear you pull up."

I didn't hear you pull up? That's what he was going to lead with?

"I parked at the far end of the lot." She sat next to him on the step. They both stared out into the dark night, lit only by the scattered lights in the parking lot and the occasional star.

"So, England, eh?" she asked after a minute.

He shook his head. "England, nay."

"What do you mean?" She turned to look at him.

He met her gray-green gaze. "I'm not going, Georgi. I was never going."

"But *Variety* …"

"Got it wrong." He picked up her hand and wrapped it in his. "I talked with the RSC months ago. It never amounted to anything."

"I shouldn't have run." A stray tear trickled down one cheek. "I should have stayed and let you explain."

"You came back. That's all that matters."

"I was just so scared. I thought …"

He gathered her close and kissed her, stopping her words and absorbing her tears with his lips.

"I know what you thought," he said when he broke the kiss and pulled back. "But look at me and believe me. I will never hurt you that way again. I'll always be up front with you, and I won't make any major decisions without talking to you first. Trust me, that's not a mistake I'm repeating any time soon."

"I believe you."

"We're in this together babe. But I can't guarantee that somewhere down the road I might be asked to go to London again. Or L.A., or Atlanta or even some podunk regional theater in West Nowhere, Kentucky." He winced at the last.

"I've always wanted to see West Nowhere," she joked. Then her eyes darkened and her tone turned serious. "I know your job is unpredictable and involves travel. It's the nature of the beast. All I ask is that we discuss it first, like you said."

"Deal. With one condition."

"What's that?"

"I want to move my home base here. To Spring Grove. It's only a few hours from New York." His heart beat triple time while he waited for her answer.

Her eyes widened. "Are you saying you want to live with me?"

"If you'll have me." He gave her a smile designed to charm her panties off. "Or I can always make my short-term rental long-term."

"I'll have you." She leaned in and placed a soft kiss on his lips. "I wouldn't subject anyone to that place long-term."

"Then we've got a deal?" He extended his hand for her to shake.

"Deal." She eyed his outstretched hand. "But I can think of a better way to finalize it than a handshake."

"Oh you can, can you?" He gathered her in again. "Are any of them legal in a public parking lot?"

"Not one."

"Then let's go." He stood and pulled her up with him.

She threw her arms around him and plastered her body to his. "Where to?"

"We'll start with your place. Or, should I say, our place." He kissed her, a deep, powerful kiss to seal the commitment they'd made. "I love you, Georgi. As long as I've got you to come home to, I'm happy."

"I love you, too, Jax. I never really stopped loving you. I'm just sorry we wasted so much time."

"It's not time wasted if it brought us here."

"And where exactly is that?" she asked, squealing as he picked her up and headed for his car.

"Together. Forever."

To My Readers:

Thank you so much for reading *Summer Stock!*

If you couldn't tell from the setting for my novella, I'm a huge theater geek. To some people, the word summer conjures images of sand and sun. To me, it screams summer theater, like the shows that are performed by amateurs and professionals around the country every year from May to September. Jax and Georgie sprung from many of the real-life showmances I've witnessed (okay, and been part of) throughout the years.

If you liked reading a romance with an arts-related theme, check out my Art of Seduction series for Harlequin Blaze. Each of the four books has some sort of connection with the arts. Like *Summer Stock*, the first book in the series, *Triple Threat*, also has a theater setting. In *Triple Time*, heroine Devin is a bartender/tattoo artist who dreams of being a painter and *Triple Dare* is photographer Ivy's story. And *Triple Score* completes the series.

I love keeping in touch with my readers. You can follow me on:

Facebook: ReginaKyleAuthor
Twitter: @Regina_Kyle1
Pinterest:ReginaKyleAutho

If you want first crack at exclusive excerpts and sneak peeks, sign up for my newsletter at my website. And for more fun stuff, like exclusive excerpts and special giveaways, you can join my readers' group, aptly named *Regina's Rabble Rousers*, on Facebook. Come play with us!

Until, then, remember, all the world's a stage, and we are merely players!

Happy Reading!

About the Author:

Regina Kyle knew she was destined to be an author when she won a writing contest at age eight with a touching tale about a squirrel and a nut pie. By day, she writes dry legal briefs, representing the state in criminal appeals. At night, she writes steamy romance with heart and humor. Her novel *Triple Dare* for Harlequin Blaze was a 2016 Booksellers' Best award winner. A lover of all things theatrical, Regina lives on the Connecticut shoreline with her husband, teenaged daughter and two melodramatic cats. When she's not writing, she's most likely singing, reading, cooking or watching bad reality television.

To keep up with her latest book news, sign up for her newsletter on her website.

ReginaKyle.com

Books by Regina Kyle

Harlequin Blaze

Triple Threat
Triple Time
Triple Dare
Triple Score

Ashland Falls Novellas

Summer Stock
Sugar Plum Seduction

Proof

73022023R00059

Made in the USA
Columbia, SC
01 July 2017